The Three Bears

ADAPTED FROM ROBERT SOUTHEY'S
"THE STORY OF THE THREE BEARS"

ILLUSTRATED BY NORMAN MESSENGER

DORLING KINDERSLEY
London • New York • Sydney • Moscow

ONCE UPON A TIME

there were Three Bears who lived together in a house in a wood.

One of them was a
Small, Wee Bear,

one was a

**Middle-sized
Bear,**

and the

third was a

**Great,
Huge Bear.**

One day, after the Three Bears had made porridge for their breakfast, they walked out into the woods while the porridge was cooling.

A little girl came to the house and peeped in at the keyhole.

Seeing nobody there, she lifted the latch and went in. The door was not locked, because the Bears were good Bears, who never suspected that anybody would harm them.

The girl was pleased to see the porridge.
If she had been good, she would have
waited for the Bears to ask her to breakfast.
But she set about helping herself.

First she tasted the
porridge of the
Great, Huge Bear,
and that was too
hot for her.

Then she tasted
the porridge of
the Middle Bear,
and that was
too cold for her.

Then she tasted the
porridge of the Small,
Wee Bear, and
that was just right.
She ate it all up.

Then the girl sat
in the chair of the
Great, Huge Bear,
and that was too
hard for her.

Then she sat in the
chair of the Middle
Bear, and that was
too soft for her.

Then she sat in the chair of the Small,
Wee Bear, and that was just right.
There she sat till the bottom of
the chair came out, and
down came hers,
plump upon
the ground.

Then the girl went upstairs into the bedroom. First she lay upon the bed of the Great, Huge Bear, but that was too high at the head for her.

Next she lay upon
the bed of the
Middle Bear, and
that was too high
at the foot for her.

Then she lay upon the bed of
the Small, Wee Bear, and
that was just right. So she
covered herself up and
fell fast asleep.

By this time the Three Bears thought their porridge would be cool enough, so they came home to breakfast.

Now the girl had left the spoon of the Great, Huge Bear standing in his porridge.

"Somebody has been at my porridge!"

said the Great, Huge Bear, in his great, rough, gruff voice.

And when the Middle Bear looked
at his, he saw that the spoon
was standing in it, too.
**"Somebody has
been at my
porridge!"**
said the Middle
Bear, in his
middle voice.

Then the Small, Wee Bear looked at his,
but the porridge was all gone.

"Somebody has been at my porridge,
and has eaten it all up!"

said the Small, Wee Bear,
in his small, wee voice.

The Three Bears began to look about them. Now the girl had not put the hard cushion straight when she rose from the chair of the Great, Huge Bear.

"Somebody has been sitting in my chair!"

said the Great, Huge Bear,
in his great, rough, gruff voice.

The girl had squatted down the soft cushion of the Middle Bear.

"Somebody has been sitting in my chair!"

said the Middle Bear, in his middle voice.

And you know what the girl
had done to the third chair.

"Somebody has been sitting in my chair,
and has sat the bottom of it out!"

said the Small, Wee Bear,
in his small, wee voice.

Then the Three Bears went
upstairs into their bedroom.
Now the girl had moved
the pillow on the Great,
Huge Bear's bed.

"Somebody has been lying in my bed!"

said the Great, Huge

Bear, in his

great, rough,

gruff voice.

And the girl had moved the bolster
on the Middle Bear's bed.
**"Somebody has been
lying in my bed!"**
said the Middle
Bear, in his
middle voice.

And when the Small, Wee Bear
came to look at his bed, there upon
the pillow was the girl's head.

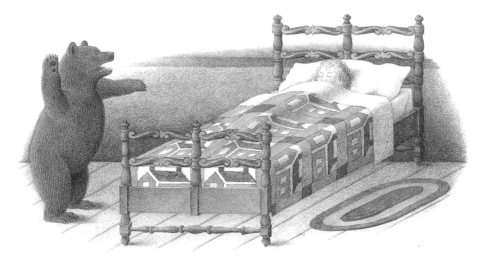

"Somebody has been lying in my bed, and here she is!"

said the Small, Wee Bear,

in his small, wee voice.

When the girl heard the small, wee voice, of the Small, Wee Bear, it woke her at once. Up she started, and when she saw the Three Bears on one side of the bed, she tumbled herself out the other, and ran to the window.

Out the girl jumped, and the Three Bears never saw anything more of her.

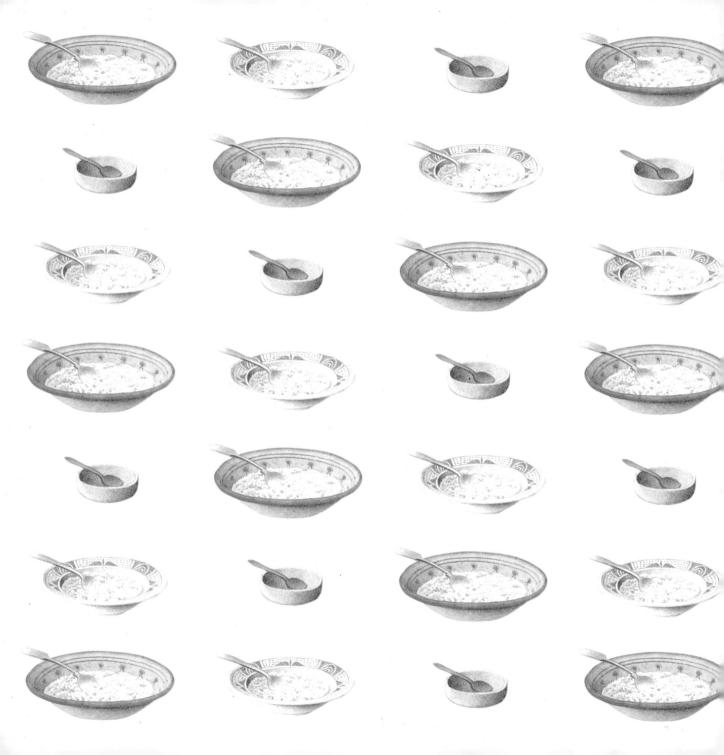